THE UNDERGROUND DWELLERS

by Emma Carlson-Berne
illustrated by Dan Whisker

a Capstone company — publishers for children

Engage Literacy is published in the UK by Raintree.
Raintree is an imprint of Capstone Global Library Limited, a company incorporated in England and Wales having its registered office at 264 Banbury Road, Oxford, OX2 7DY – Registered company number: 6695582

www.raintree.co.uk

Illustration copyright © Capstone/Dan Whisker

Editorial credits
Gina Kammer, editor; Rich Parker, designer; Katy LaVigne, production specialist

21 20 19 18 17
10 9 8 7 6 5 4 3 2 1
Printed and bound in the United Kindgom.

The Underground Dwellers

ISBN: 978 1 4747 4659 5

CONTENTS

Chapter 1
Return to the world. 4

Chapter 2
The sun's danger. 14

Chapter 3
Into the shelter. 24

Chapter 4
Endless night. 28

Chapter 5
Hope from the beavers 34

Chapter 6
A new life together 42

Chapter 1

RETURN TO THE WORLD

"Dig! Come on, everyone, dig!" Isaiah called from in front of Miriam. She panted and clawed at the soil with her fingers. Behind her, she could hear Chen and Davis scrambling and clawing, too. They were almost at the top of the tunnel. The floodwaters thundered below them. Their underground home was flooded. They had only just escaped drowning, and now they could never go back.

The only way out was up. The old tunnel was Isaiah's idea – he always had good ones. Years ago, the whole community had used this tunnel when everyone had to leave their homes and go underground to live. They had waited out storms more and more often in the caves. But The Disaster of 3053 had been a big one. It had destroyed their part of Earth, and after that they didn't leave the caves. No one could breathe the ashy air, and only those who had already begun to adapt to living underground could survive. Miriam could hardly remember what living above ground was like.

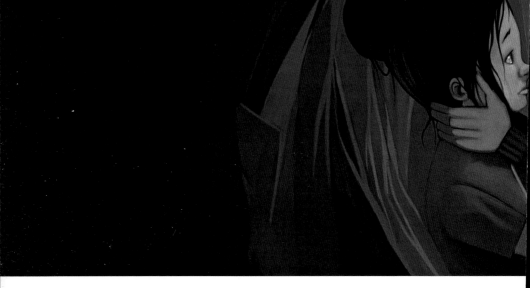

Almost everyone else had left a month ago to explore the surface. They wanted to see if they could live on Earth again – instead of in earth. But Miriam, Isaiah, Davis and Chen had to stay behind. They were the youngest of the group. The adults said the mission would be too dangerous for them. "I'll be back soon," Miriam remembered her mother saying. Mum had held her close, and Miriam had pressed up against her. "You can stay here, with the other children your age. You're just too young to come with me. It would be too hard for you."

"Do you have to go?" Miriam had whispered to her. She tried to hold back her tears.

"Yes, I do," Mum had said gently. "The others need me. All of us in the group have to help each other. It's the only way we can survive." She had turned Miriam's face up to hers. "Listen to me, my darling. We'll come back for you. Wait for me. Until then, help each other. Stay together."

Then they left. But no one ever came back. Something had gone wrong up there, on the surface. After four weeks, Miriam knew. The others knew, too – she could see it in their faces. No one was coming, and now they were alone.

Their food was running out. They couldn't wait any longer. But just as they were making their plans to journey to the surface, the floodwaters came, thundering through the caves that had been their home. The raging black water swept away the boxes of food, their jumpers and socks – everything they had. Miriam lost her only picture of Mum. They had only barely escaped up into the tunnel themselves.

Isaiah had leapt up to a high ledge near the top of the cave and shouted to the others to do the same. Now they were digging up, digging for fresh air – and they were almost there.

Suddenly, Isaiah shouted, "I think I can see the sky!"

Miriam clawed harder at the mud. The air was becoming lighter. Then, she saw it – a tiny patch of dark-blue sky. "I can see it, too!" she screamed.

With their muscles burning, fingernails full of mud, they broke through the surface. "We did it!" cried Chen.

"Finally," Davis grumbled.

Half in the hole, half out, Miriam squinted in the light that suddenly blinded her. After a while, she opened her eyes a crack and gazed around her. The sky was navy-blue with specks of a few stars, streaked with pink in the east. It must have been just before dawn. They were somewhere in the woods, with leaves and shrubs covering the ground, towering trees and a small lake ahead. Nothing looked familiar. It looked like The Disaster was over, but not much was left of the woods. The blackened trees were still standing, but their leaves had gone. Here and there green shoots were breaking through the ashy ground.

And there were no signs of any other humans.

Chapter 2

THE SUN'S DANGER

Miriam shivered in the cool air. It was hard to see. Even in the little bit of light from the sunrise, Miriam squinted against the glare. Her eyes were no longer used to the light. "Come on!" Isaiah shouted to the others. "We have to make some kind of shelter. When the sun comes up, we'll all be roasted if we don't." He was already hunting along the ground, picking up big branches.

Miriam's whole body felt heavy. Tears built up in her throat. First, The Disaster came. Then, the others left. Now, the flood. Everything was lost. Everything felt hopeless.

As if she could read Miriam's thoughts, Chen suddenly let out a loud sob. She crumpled to the ground and covered her head with her hands. "Oh! No! No! No!" she wailed.

Davis just turned his back on them all and walked away to the nearest tree. He pressed his forehead to the bark and stood there, with his head bowed.

Miriam wanted to comfort Chen but she felt frozen. How would they live without food or clothing? What if she never saw her mother's face again?

"Come on!" Isaiah shouted. He looked scared and angry. "We have to build a shelter! The sun is rising! We'll all be roasted."

Miriam looked down at her arms. They appeared ghostly pale. Isaiah's were, too – and so were Chen's and Davis's. Years of underground living had removed the colour from her skin and left it as white as the mushrooms that grew in their cave.

Fear shook Miriam out of her grief. Isaiah was right. When the sun rose, they would burn straight away because their skin wasn't used to it. They needed a shelter. She ran over and helped Isaiah drag a big branch from under a tree.

Chen raised her head. She wiped her eyes. "I'll help, too," she said and got to her feet.

"Davis, get over here! Help us lift this!" Isaiah shouted. But Davis just slid down until he was crouched against a tree, his arms wrapped around his wet shirt, shivering.

"No. I'm too cold," he chattered.

"We're all cold," Miriam told him. "And just as wet as you. But Isaiah is right – we have to have a shelter. Look." She held out her white arm. "The sun will burn us when it comes up."

Davis put his head down on his knees. "When I warm up, I'll help." He didn't move from the tree.

"Hurry!" Isaiah shouted. "We have to get under cover before the sun rises!"

"Chen, help me!" Miriam ordered. She lifted a log to balance against the one Isaiah was lifting.

Panting, they pushed branches together as quickly as they could until the structure looked a little bit like a tepee. It had tall branches leaning against each other in a cone shape. Miriam didn't think it looked very strong, though. Even as they stood back, a branch fell over and the whole structure nearly toppled.

"Whoa!" Isaiah darted forwards and pushed the branch back into place. The sun started peeking over the horizon. Miriam could feel the first light on her skin. It felt hot – too hot. She squinted. The others were squinting, too. Miriam glanced at Davis and noticed his eye colour had faded from blue until they were almost all white. Isaiah's were a pale brown. Miriam could only guess what her green eyes looked like now.

The rising sun felt like a torch shining
in her eyes. She looked down at her arms.
Already her skin was turning pink. She reached
over and pressed a finger on Chen's arm.
It left a mark – ten minutes in the sun and
they were already getting sunburned. This
shelter had to protect them if they were going
to survive.

Chapter 3

INTO THE SHELTER

"Hurry!" Isaiah shouted. They dived for the shelter. It was hard to see with their pale eyes. Miriam squeezed in between the branches as everyone piled in behind her. Davis rose quickly and pushed past Chen, trying to get in. His leg bumped the branches, and in an instant, the whole shelter collapsed like a pile of toothpicks.

"No!" Isaiah shouted. "Davis! We needed that!" The sun was fully up now. The heat and light were white-hot. They were all squinting, barely able to see.

"It was too small!" Davis shouted back. "You should have made it bigger."

"You should have helped!" Isaiah shouted.

Miriam heard her mother's voice in her head. Help each other. Stay together. "Stop!" she burst out. "Please. Don't fight." She put her hands out to stop each of the boys.

The sun shining through the clearing was blazing hot. They could hardly see with their pale eyes. Chen pulled her short-sleeved t-shirt over her arms to protect them.

"Here, the water is clear," she waved them over. "We can have a drink."

They each knelt by the lake edge where there was a tiny bit of shade. Miriam scooped the cold water up in her hands and slurped.

Chen pointed out towards the lake, squinting hard. "Look out there."

Miriam squinted, too. It looked like four brown lumps moving around in the water. "Are those animals?" she asked.

"Beavers, I think. They keep swimming around with twigs in their mouths," Isaiah said. A harsh red colour had spread across his face. Sunburn. Isaiah gazed at the pile of sticks that had been their shelter, then at the hot sun overhead.

"Come on, everyone. Let's try to get some sleep," he said. "We can try building again in the evening and then try to find something to eat."

They lay down in an uncomfortable row with the branches piled over them. The ground was hard and hot. The sun beat through the branches. Miriam was exhausted after their night in the tunnel, but she couldn't sleep. Her skin was scorching, her stomach twisted with hunger and Isaiah's foot was almost in her face. If only there were leaves on the trees, they could find more shade! But The Disaster had taken care of that.

Chapter 4

ENDLESS NIGHT

Hunger was tearing at Miriam's insides when she rose at sunset from under the branches. Chen looked over from a large pile of leaves she'd plucked from the tree shoots peeking from the ground. Her face was bright red with sunburn.

A metre or so away, Isaiah was already struggling to prop the branches of their shelter up again. But they kept toppling over.

"Ooohhhrr!" Davis opened his eyes and sat up. His face was red and puffy with sunburn, too. "I'm so hungry!" He rolled over and buried his face in his arms.

"Everyone! Come and help me! Let's build this shelter – then we can look for food once the sun's gone down," Isaiah called. Miriam and Chen scrambled to their feet, but Davis just remained face down on the ground.

"Come on, Davis!" Miriam nudged him with her foot.

He didn't move.

The shelter would not stay up. After several more attempts trying different ways to put up the poles, Miriam ended up with a bruise on her arm from being hit by a branch. But they finally had something they could use for shelter. All of their eyes were pouring with tears from the strong sun. Chen's face was the worst. Her sunburn had become so bad that she'd broken out in a rash of tiny blisters. Davis stayed under the tree in the deepest shade with his head on his arms, which rested on his knees.

Later in the black night, the clouds rolled in. There had been no time to find food before the storm was upon them. The four huddled in their cramped shelter while thunder boomed through the trees and the wind raced loudly. Lightning flashed, showing their faces in strange blue-white.

"Oh, no," Isaiah said as the first raindrops started.

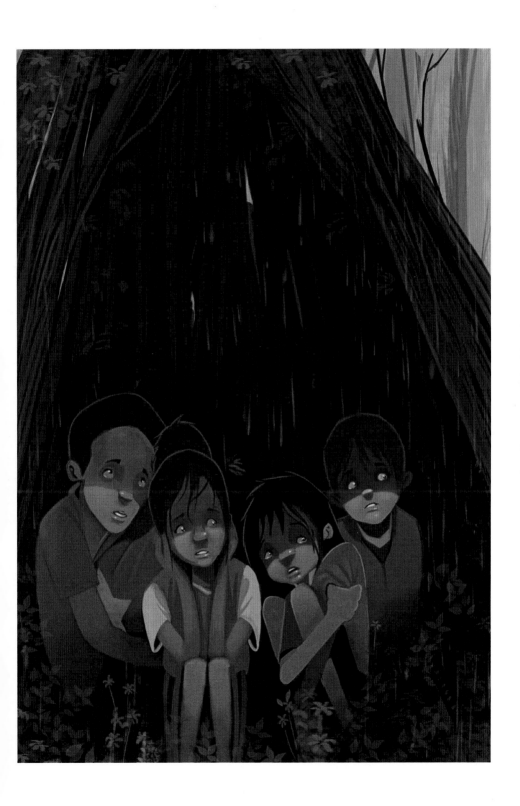

Quickly the pattering grew faster and faster until the downpour roared through the branches. It soaked the shaky tepee they'd made. Miriam was soaked through. Her hair was plastered to the sides of her face. She shivered wildly.

Davis suddenly reared up from the ground. "This . . . shelter . . . stinks!" he grunted and kicked the branch nearest him. With a clatter that could barely be heard over the loud thunder, the shelter fell over into a pile of branches again.

"Davis!" Isaiah shouted. He pulled a large branch off Chen. "You haven't helped us for even one minute since we came above ground! And now you've wrecked the shelter!" His voice was angry. Miriam could tell he was crying, though she couldn't see much through the mess of wet branches that surrounded them now.

Miriam thought that night would never end.

Chapter 5

HOPE FROM THE BEAVERS

As the sun rose, they collapsed on the edge of the lake to rest. The tepee was still a pile of sticks. Chen returned to her large stack of leaves. Lazily, Miriam watched her cutting a thin slit in each one with a sharp twig. But she was too tired and too foggy with hunger and painful sunburn to ask what she was doing.

Miriam stared blankly at the lake, which she could see now was actually a small pond. The beavers were there again, swimming and climbing up and down a large mound of sticks and mud at the end of the pond. At the other end, a pile of sticks and branches spread across the pond. Miriam realised that it must be the beavers' dam. They'd built it and flooded part of the forest to make themselves a pond. She remembered learning about that back in school – when there was school. She had had a family, too, she reminded herself, and a home.

There were two large beavers and two small ones – the parents and their kits. Miriam watched the biggest one swim over to the edge of the pond, climb out and waddle over to a small tree. He snipped off a large twig. He swam over to the big stick mound, with his brown head above the water, then climbed out onto the mound. As the children watched, the beaver pushed the twig into the mound.

"That's their lodge," Isaiah whispered. He was watching the beavers, too, his eyes glazed with tiredness.

"What is it?" Chen asked. She was stripping long, thin strings of bark off a pile of small branches now.

"Their house," Miriam explained. She was starting to remember other things about beavers. "We learned about them at school. They make a big mound of sticks and mud, and they build chambers inside. One is for eating, and one is for sleeping and having babies. The entrance is underwater. That helps protect them from predators."

Miriam looked down at her arms in the pre-dawn darkness. Tiny blisters had risen up on her angry red skin. She didn't know how much time they had before one of them became unwell with sun poisoning. It wasn't much time – she knew that.

The kits were following their parents' lead and snipping off branches, too. Then, the female beaver dove down into the water. She came up with something dripping from her paws. Miriam squinted. "What's she carrying?" she asked.

"It looks like grass and mud," Isaiah answered slowly. He didn't sound as if he cared. He sat propped up against a tree trunk, his face streaked with mud.

Miriam wanted to weep when she thought of another day of trying to sleep under the collapsed branches. Another day was coming, full of hunger and sunburn and headaches from the sun. Miriam didn't think she could bear it.

Tiredly, Miriam watched the female beaver dive under the water again. She came up from the pond with another armful of muddy grass. She swam to the edge of the lodge and packed the mud in among the branches. Then the male beaver stuck another twig straight into the mud. How solid their home looked!

Suddenly, Miriam sat up. Mud. The beavers were using branches and sticks. Just like them. But they were using something else, too. Mud. Plaster. The mud was plaster. The grass kept the mud strong. The beavers were making their house solid and watertight.

"Chen! Isaiah!" Miriam shouted. She jumped to her feet as the others looked at her in surprise. Even Davis lifted his head. "Hurry! We need to get some mud!"

Chapter 6

A NEW LIFE TOGETHER

"Mud?" Isaiah looked puzzled.

"And grass. Muddy grass." As fast as she could, Miriam explained.

"Let's get to work!" Isaiah cried with his old energy.

"Wait!" Chen held up her hand. She trotted to a nearby stump and retrieved something lying on the top. "I made these for us. They'll help our eyes. Sometimes we'll need to work during the day, I thought. Not just at night. So when we do . . ." She held up four pairs of big leaves with slits in the middles, strung together with tree bark. They were like leaf glasses – or sunglasses, Miriam realised.

"Chen, thank you!" Miriam tried hers on and looked through the little slit. The cool shade soothed her aching eyes. "How did you think of these?"

Chen smiled. "I remembered the picture I saw of Arctic explorers wearing wooden eye shields with slits to block the glare of the sun on the snow. I thought leaves might work for us." She looked towards Davis. "I made some for you, too," she told him gently.

Davis rose slowly and came over to them. Without saying anything, he accepted his leaf goggles. Then he took a deep breath. "I . . . I want to help. With the mud and the shelter."

While everyone stared at him, mouths open, he went on. "I mean . . . there are four of the beavers. And there are four of us. They're all working together and . . . well, we should too – shouldn't we?" He offered a shy smile.

Help each other. Stay together. Miriam could feel her mother's words within her. "That's right!" she told Davis and hugged him. "Thank you, Davis. We need every pair of hands."

The eastern sky was getting pinker. Sunrise was coming. Wearing their leaf goggles, Miriam, Chen, Davis and Isaiah ran back and forth from the pond to the shelter. They wove thin branches between the thick ones, like a basket. Then, they plugged the many holes with a mixture of twisted grass and sticky mud. They smoothed the top to shed the rain. Miriam paused, smiling at the beavers in thanks.

When they had finally finished, the morning sun was sending rays across the pond. Isaiah took a deep breath. "Let's try it out." One by one, they crawled inside. It was cool, dark and a little bit damp inside – like their cave.

Miriam peered out through her leaf glasses and noticed a group of people trudging towards them carrying spears and heavy sacks. She recognised her mother helping someone walk. "Look!" she shouted. Everyone saw and cheered.

They had learned to live underground – now they could all learn how to live in this new, different world, too. The shelter was only the beginning of their work – of their life. But it was the beginning they needed to learn how to work together.